11.00

AIRMAIL

Naomi Bulger

iUniverse, Inc.
Bloomington

AIRMAIL

Copyright © 2011 by Naomi Bulger

All rights reserved. No part of this book may be used or reproduced by any means, graphic, electronic, or mechanical, including photocopying, recording, taping or by any information storage retrieval system without the written permission of the publisher except in the case of brief quotations embodied in critical articles and reviews.

iUniverse books may be ordered through booksellers or by contacting:

iUniverse
1663 Liberty Drive
Bloomington, IN 47403
www.iuniverse.com
1-800-Authors (1-800-288-4677)

Because of the dynamic nature of the Internet, any web addresses or links contained in this book may have changed since publication and may no longer be valid. This is a work of fiction. All of the characters, names, incidents, organizations, and dialogue in this novel are either the products of the author's imagination or are used fictitiously..

ISBN: 978-1-4502-3549-5 (pbk)
ISBN: 978-1-4502-3550-1 (ebk)
ISBN: 978-1-4502-3551-8 (hbk)

Printed in the United States of America
iUniverse rev. date: 3/1/11

CHAPTER 1

The old man opened the stranger's letter and started to read. You couldn't tell just by looking whether the tension around his eyes was anticipation or just irritation. His hand shook as he unfolded the page, but that could as easily have been age as excitement.

A U.S. penny, dated 1982, fell out, as did a cup-stained, unbranded paper napkin with the words "the coffee is terrible" written across it in blue ink. The ink ran at the edges. There was always some kind of memento like this. The stranger had, as usual, seemed to scribble on any paper that came to hand. This time it was the disemboweled airmail envelope itself, written on inside and out.

"Dear Mr. G. L. Solomon," it began. That was the old man's name.

I am being followed. How silly to be afraid of a fat-bottomed woman in a pink, velour tracksuit. She's everywhere I go—never behind me, always in front. But I do mean *always* in front.

The first time I saw her was outside a downtown bar called La Esquina. That's a Latin-style place that used to be cool, and I read about it in *Harper's* before I came. Supposedly, men would dance with you and buy you cocktails, but in reality, it's too crowded to breathe properly, let alone dance, and all we do is sweat and buy our own damned expensive drinks. Oh, and there's a *law* against *dancing* in this town. Seriously! Can you believe it? New York is insane.

Anyway, I went outside for a little break, and there was a chubby black lady in a pink tracksuit having a cigarette. I noticed her because tracksuits aren't exactly standard La Esquina gear. We shared one of those half smiles—you know—when you don't know somebody but there's something there and you keep eye contact longer than usual? I went back inside, and later I saw her dancing crazily (and illegally) in the back of the bar.

So it's two days later, and I'm at Magnolia, which is this place in the Village where you can get a hundred different types of cupcakes. The lady is already lining up for her cupcake and tea, and I recognize her straight away. She's even wearing the same pink tracksuit.

Airmail

On Sunday afternoon, I'm catching the subway with two friends, and we're heading up to see the Yankees play the Tampa Devil Rays from the eleven-dollar seats out in the bleachers. I notice her as we go to board the train, just in front of us, and we end up sitting three seats down from her. She's wearing a Yankees cap, just as we all are. And she's still wearing the pink tracksuit! I don't look sideways, so I don't catch her eye, but I know she's watching me. It's starting to freak me out. We lose her at the stadium, but I know she is there somewhere, probably in the bleachers.

Back home in SoHo, I see her pink tracksuit backside in the weekend shopping crowd just a little ahead of me. Twice. I am definitely being followed. And I have my suspicions, but I don't really know why.

Yours,

Anouk

The old man frowned momentarily. Then he drained the last of the whiskey, warm now, which sat on the small table beside his armchair. He carefully folded the envelope back up, pulled a shoebox from under the green fabric trimming on the armchair, and placed the letter, the penny, and the napkin inside it. Already in the box was a small pile of letters in the same handwriting.

From a faded, hand-tinted portrait in a cheap, gilt frame that hung slightly askew on the wallpaper, a prettyish young woman in old-fashioned clothes watched the old man. She watched him as he eased himself out of the chair and walked slowly into the kitchen, flipped the kettle on, put a tea bag in a china teacup without bothering with the saucer, and lit a cigarette while he waited for the kettle to boil. The old man did not so much as glance in the direction of the portrait.

It was 10:00 AM on a Tuesday.

* * *

The old man finished the cigarette, was down to the last sip of his cup of tea, and thought about heading into town to purchase his regular groceries. On the other side of the world, Anouk and a small group of new friends got up to leave Café Lalo on the Upper West Side on Manhattan, New York. Her stomach was full of berries, her mouth tasted of sugar, and it had grown dark outside while she ate. Someone had just told a joke, and they all laughed as they stepped out of the café. Anouk later discovered a piece of blackberry caught front and center in her teeth that nobody told her about.

Just ahead, waddling out of the same café and down the steps and into the twilight, she caught a glimpse of pink. Velour tracksuit. She knew it! Anouk grabbed the arm of the friend nearest to her, Sarah, and pointed with the other hand. She asked, "Do you see that woman over there? The stalker! She's here!" Sarah looked around, swiveling her head in completely the wrong direction. "Other way! The other way! Do you see her?" But the woman had disappeared into the crowd.

It was so frustrating. It always seemed to happen that way. Everybody missed the woman except Anouk.

And as the group formed questions, Anouk felt the familiar isolation begin to settle heavily among the berries.

Who could blame them for not understanding? Who would be afraid of a fat backside, phantom or flesh, in a tacky velour tracksuit? The woman hardly had the physique of a paid assassin. And to an impartial observer, it would appear that Anouk was doing the stalking, not the other way around. Yet the situation felt sinister, and Anouk felt alone. Pink Tracksuit didn't look back as she disappeared into the early evening of the tree-lined street among the café goers and the children playing marbles by porch light on the smooth steps of the classic brownstones. But Anouk could feel her eyes.

An hour later, alone in her tiny boardinghouse room, Anouk began to pace. Inside her head, she retraced her steps since landing at JFK International in the muggy late July—the people she had met, her regular haunts. Scouring her memory for a glimpse of anyone who may somehow be connected to the eccentric spy.

She searched for the point at which her path first crossed with the Pink Tracksuit's, or for the moment when the daily exercise of her new identity may have unintentionally left open a window to her old life.

A sudden thought occurred to Anouk, and she rushed to the top drawer in the dresser by the bed. With relief, she saw that her passport, the only document in the room containing her real name, appeared undisturbed. She pulled it out, flipped through it, put it back, and closed the drawer. Then, remembering a childhood episode of *The Famous Five*, she found some talcum powder in the bathroom cabinet. Very lightly, almost imperceptibly, she dusted the passport with the powder so that it would reveal future fingerprints. For a moment, she felt clever and smug.

Then she thought about her old life again, a life that was now inseparable from memories of him. Abruptly, Anouk sat down on the edge of the bed and started to cry.

CHAPTER 2

In the Sydney and Greater Metropolitan White Pages, he was listed as Mr. G. L. Solomon, 02 9218 5068. But nobody called the number. G. L. stood for G—— L——.

His favorite things were as follows: single-malt whiskey, Steve McQueen movies, and gingersnap cookies.

His pet hates were as follows: the way the teacup rattled in the saucer when he picked it up, domestic cats, processed cheese, and washing detergent commercials.

The old man never looked at the crooked photograph on the wall of his lounge room. It is possible that he had forgotten it even existed. But the woman in the photograph watched everything, and she waited.

On Wednesday at 9:00 AM, still in his dressing gown and slippers, he pulled the trash can out to the curb in case he forgot later that night. Shuffling back up the path to the unit, he mock-hissed at number five's fat, earless tabby cat.

At 10:00 AM, the old man put *Fishing World* magazine down on a pile of dried and yellowing handwritten notes. He barely saw the notepaper through the years the pages had rested on that very table. But from her place in the frame over the wallpaper, the portrait could read the top page of the faded handwriting: "Aust greats story idea: Bradman, D. Ave 99.94; Phar Lap. 37 from 51; Goolagong, E. 14 Grand Slam." There were many more statistics written on the dusty paper, but no story put flesh on their bones. The fading lines on the sheets underneath, if only the portrait could have seen them, remained blank.

The old man flipped the kettle on and lit a cigarette while he waited for the kettle to boil. He pulled out a teacup but not a saucer, set it on the table, and had another drag on the cigarette.

At noon, freshly showered, still with droplets of water in his gray hair and talcum powder between his toes, he made a ham, chutney, and cheese sandwich. He sat down at the kitchen table to eat; but before he started, he seemed to think better of the situation and got up again. He took two gingersnaps out of the cupboard, which he placed on the side of the plate for after. Then he sat back down and took a bite of the sandwich, which was cut in rectangles, not triangles.

At 2:30 PM, *Days of Our Lives* was on the television. He despised it, but it was insidious, and it was his evil addiction.

At 3:30 PM, he turned the television off. An ancient camera sat on top of the TV, coated in dust and moisture patches, its lens cap long since disappeared and its leather strap gathering mold. For the next half hour, the old man looked at the old camera on the blank television.

He thought about his youth.

Four o'clock in the afternoon was post time. As soon as the mailman motored away up the hill, the old man shuffled out to the boxes. He opened his and found nothing. Closed it. He opened it again and felt around inside in case a letter was lying flat in the box, and he missed it the first time. Nothing. Closed the box. Gathered all the detritus of junk mail that lay scattered over the top of the boxes and sticking out of the slots and on the ground around them, picked it all up, and took it to the recycle bin.

Hissed and stomped at the tabby on his way back inside, sending it scuttling into the laundry to hide.

At 6:00 PM, under the watchful eyes of the portrait in the crooked frame but not once glancing in her direction, the old man put down *Fishing World* and stood up, stretched, shuffled to the kitchen, and put a saucepan on to boil.

He plopped in five hot dogs, mixed up some powdered mashed potato with milk and water, sliced some fresh cucumber and tomato, and arranged them on a plate. He took a bottle of ketchup out of the fridge to allow it to warm up to room temperature while he cooked and set the kitchen table for one. There was a place mat, a coaster for his glass of orange juice, a knife, a fork, and a paper napkin like the one the stranger had sent him with the coffee stains.

At 7:00 PM, he finished washing up and turned on *ABC News*.

Soldiers were mistreating prisoners of war.

Bushfire season had started early in the nation's capital—two suburbs evacuated but no houses lost.

The prime minister looked likely to campaign the next election on homeland security.

The Greens were bickering.

At 8:30 PM, he watched *Who Wants to be a Millionaire?* The old man did—and knew he could be if he ever went on the show.

Add to his pet hates uneducated twerps who went on quiz shows with no adequate comprehension of sports, history, politics, science, Pythagorean theorey, or common sense.

At 10:00 PM, he bent and touched the air four inches above his toes ten times, trembled through ten push-ups, and, knees bent and hands behind his head, painfully crunched into ten sit-ups. Then he poured a shot-sized glass of whiskey, no ice, and drained it in one swallow. He brushed his teeth, changed into his pajamas, and was in bed by 10:30 PM, where he slept like a baby for precisely ten hours.

There was a telephone on his bedside table, but it did not ring. Each morning to evening was the same. The days followed one after the other without feature or change.

On Thursday at 9:00 AM, still in his pajamas, the old man dragged in the trash can, smiling gently as the fat tabby ran in fear from the bin's rumbling. He finished off *Fishing World*, made his tea, and had his one cigarette at 10:00 AM. Then he showered, started on *Fisherman's Catch,* and enjoyed a ham, cheese, and chutney sandwich at noon. Victor was up to his old tricks on *Days of Our Lives,* and at 4:05 PM, with the smell of two-stroke from the mailman's scooter still in the air, the mailbox was empty.

He read some more, watched a little television, and cooked a microwave dinner at 6:00 PM. He was in bed by 10:30 PM, following his personally designed mix of exercise and alcohol. All day, the telephone didn't ring. All day, the woman in the portrait watched the old man, and the old man didn't look at anything new or anything old.

On Friday at 4:00 PM, it was post time.

He put down *Fisherman's Catch* and shuffled to the mailbox in the wake of the two-stroke. Opened the box. Nothing. Felt inside to be sure. Nothing. Closed it, cleaned up the junk mail that was starting to accumulate again, and went back inside to his reading. No telephone calls that day.

On Saturday at 4:00 PM, there was no post, but he was aware.

Saturday, 6:00 PM. Today was day fourteen. Day fourteen was a good day because, every day fourteen, the old man would wake from his hibernation.

He showered late, and he shaved while his skin was still warm, carefully and slowly dragging the blade in the same direction as the growth of his beard.

He let out an audible "Ooh!" as he slapped on the aftershave, and, hair still dripping and talcum powder between his toes, he ambled to the closet.

The old man's stomach knew the time, and it grumbled, but he ignored it and pulled out his olive green trousers with the permanent press crease in the front and an Italian leather belt. He took out a short-sleeved collared shirt, already smooth from the ironing he did every Sunday afternoon after doing laundry, carefully tucked it in, and embarked on his second life.

On day fourteen, the old man left the house with a spring in his step—no shuffling. There was also no tabby in sight. He crossed the road, walked briskly up the hill without panting, and had a wait of about one minute, according to his watch, for the 380 bus into the city. He got off at Central Station and took another bus, which let him off on the corner of Crown and Liverpool streets. He almost jogged down the hill to Stanley Street, where he could hear voices and smell spaghetti Bolognese from three blocks away.

Here, every pension week Saturday, the old man became a young man without routine or chutney or television or framed photographs. Every second Saturday night, he was a loved and respected man, roughly hugged and shoved and punched and welcomed by the Italian Old Guard inhabiting Stanley Street.

"Prego!" Mario, the barman, yelled and poured the old man a grappa without being asked. They chuckled, argued good-naturedly about nothing much, and then they ambled outside to enjoy the late sunset at the metal tables outside of Mario's café, The Colonnade.

Soon, a cigarette hung loosely from the old man's lips, and he was unperturbed by the ash that gently littered his shirt.

Large, yellow umbrellas which, in an effort to brighten the outdoor tables, Mario had ordered the week before, shaded the old man and Mario from the evening sun. Inside, The Colonnade was a room in need of paint that housed a pool table of dubious descent, two ancient pinball machines, and a jukebox. Further in, unknown to daylight or hygiene, was a scattering of plain wooden tables and chairs. At one table, two taxi drivers made less-than-legal insurance plans. Where three tables had been pushed together, two actors of international fame met with a handful of unknowns for their weekly Narcotics Anonymous gathering. A poet sat alone in the corner, listening and writing. The waiters served up coffee, well made on a bad machine, and lemon and pistachio and vanilla gelati—unsurpassable flavors—made by Mario's lady friend Julia.

Outside where the two old men smoked, clouds spread lazily across the warm sky. Ancient Gino sauntered over from the pub across the road, eased himself into a chair the other side of the old man, and lit a cigarette. The three of them watched rain gather over the street in friendly silence.

Bats flapped low in the Sydney dusk, fooled by the light rain into thinking the clouds were night. From a distance, each was a silhouette, black and evil shaped, sharp. But as they drifted over The Colonnade, the old man could see the fur on their underbellies, tiny feet tucked back, wings translucent, almost blending with the storm clouds (blue, gray, white, he noticed). They emerged in haphazard bunches from The Domain park, flying crookedly, still groggy with sleep. In drowsy formation, they swooped around the tall buildings, crossed William Street without waiting for the green, aimed straight along Yurong and Riley, and then made a left into Stanley Street. It began to rain.

The men moved to a table just inside by the window and behind the pool table. Outside, all the restaurants tilted the outdoor chairs against the outdoor tables to allow the water to run off. Upstairs at The Colonnade, pasta was sold for five dollars a plate. Friends shared wine and cola and pasta as the evening settled, and waiters lit candles on every table.

At the corner of Stanley Street and Crown, the now wide-awake bats turned right, aiming, no doubt, for Oxford Street, where their radars revealed the nightlife was best.

CHAPTER 3

While the old man messily slurped up spaghetti, smoked cigarettes without ashing in a tray, and appreciated Mario's homemade red wine by the mugful, Anouk should have been sleeping. But she wasn't. It was 4:00 AM in downtown Manhattan, and she sat up on the foldout mattress of her boardinghouse, writing. At this moment, she shared the bed with her landlady's two Burmese cats, who had won their place on the thin mattress through sheer, bloody-minded persistence.

She was still a little lightheaded from a local barman's magic mojitos, but matters were starting to clear. And before she could sleep, she needed to write Mr. G. L. a letter. She'd run out of writing paper again, but she still had a few pages left in her sketchbook, and she wrote on those without planning or forethought.

Dear G. L.,

I can't sleep. I wonder if you ever have that trouble. It's possible it's a guilty conscience that's stopping me—that's what they say in the movies. Or too much on my mind. Or too much excitement in my life. I've had enough alcohol tonight to put me out for a week, so there must be something pretty strong getting in the way.

Remember Pink Tracksuit Lady? I've figured her out. Well, at least, I've narrowed her down (so to speak). Because she's still around, here's all I can think of: she wants something I have. Well, yeah, I know that's obvious, but I mean, something other than money or valuable belongings, which I don't have. Like a thriller movie—maybe there's something I have that I don't know I have, but she knows I have it, and she wants it. Badly. In the movies, it would be a number, or a poem, which is the key to her power or wealth. What I can't figure out, though, is why she hasn't made her move yet. What is she waiting for? So …

And why doesn't anyone else see her? I mean, it's not like she's invisible or even hard to miss. She's no ghost or anything like that. It's just that every time I point her out to my friends, she manages to blend into the crowds. And what's with the pink tracksuit? It feels creepy. So …

Well, if you don't hear from me in a while, you know I've probably been beaten up somewhere by a big ass in a pink tracksuit for money or answers I don't have. You probably think that because I go out all the time, I must have money to burn, especially in this city. But that sort of stuff is all about who you know, and how the people you know think they know you, if you know what I mean. It's all about illusion.

A boy named Joseph buys my drinks at Café Dante. That's this place with a lot of rules. You know, things like 'no dogs' and 'no laptop computers' and 'cash only,' et cetera, et cetera. It's where Bob Dylan used to go to write poetry and music and be inspired, so I go there to soak him up. So does Joseph. He has bushy, strawberry-blond sideburns that almost grow into his mouth. Joseph is an intellectual with a capital *I*, and he writes philosophical papers for his class at NYU that I don't understand. Sometimes, when I read them, I frown and look thoughtful and make "hmph" sounds or suddenly yell, "*Yes*!" and startle the people in the café so that he thinks that he and I are on the same page.

He tries to engage me to discuss his papers after I have read them, but I tell him that his words need to "gestate in my mind" before I will be ready to discuss. That's held him off so far.

> Joseph thinks I am imagining things with the Pink
> Tracksuit. He has never seen her, even though she's
> drunk coffee in Dante, alone, twice while we were
> there, leaving just before us. She disappeared into the
> crowd on the pavement before I could point her out.
> If I get too worked up, Joseph buys me another drink,
> which he can hardly afford because he is a student,
> but he always seems to have just enough money and
> no more.

Anouk put the pen down and chewed at the end for a while. She fell asleep.

The following night, Anouk ate dinner at the counter in a diner on Sixth Avenue. She ordered a plate of buffalo wings and a leaf salad with cheese.

Later, when Anouk returned home to the boardinghouse, she took out her letter to Mr. G. L. and wrote across the bottom:

> They are obsessed with revolting, runny, orange
> cheese. It's smeared over every bloody meal.

Then she folded the letter, slipped it into an envelope along with a box of matches from the diner, sealed it, and put it aside to mail the next morning.

That night, though, once again, Anouk couldn't sleep. She read a fashion magazine for a little while, and then she sat up in bed with the two cats and watched reruns of *The Bachelor* on TV. There was a knock at the door.

Airmail

Anouk didn't answer because it was well past midnight, and she wasn't expecting visitors. The walls in the boardinghouse were thin, and the knock could well have been on a door across the hall.

There was a second knock, and one of the cats woke up and started chasing a discarded marble across the dusty floorboards. Through the peephole, Anouk could see the top of a short, dark head and a glimpse of pink velour. She felt the orange cheese rise in her throat. Slowly, quietly, she stepped away from the door and sat down on the edge of the mattress, absently stroking the other cat. *The Bachelor* went into an ad break. Anouk sat still while the ads finished, and when the program came back on, she didn't move during the whole time it took Bachelor Randy to give six red roses to six blonde clones. There had been one more knock during an ad for asthma medication, which she had ignored, and no more. Then, just as *The Bachelor* gave way to a show about celebrities playing practical jokes on one another, she heard a shuffle behind the door. It was a stealthy scratching that sounded like leather softly sliding on floorboards.

Enough. Anouk closed her eyes, held her breath, and counted to ten. She waited two uneasy beats after reaching ten, and then she ran to the door and opened it with a rush of wind. Nobody was there. But leaning out into the hall, she saw an ankle in pink disappear toward the elevators.

For a moment, Anouk thought about following her. She thought about running after the pink ankle to see whether it was indeed attached to an overweight woman with a penchant for velour, as she suspected. She thought about loudly confronting the woman, forcibly dragging her from sinister surveillance into the world of flesh and blood and reality, ending a reverse chase that was gradually becoming her constant fear.

But she did not. Instead, Anouk closed and locked the door, sat on the edge of the bed, and watched the celebrity candid camera program, filling her mind with the welcome vacuity of television until dawn.

* * *

But if Anouk *had* run after the pink ankle, she would not have had to go far. The ankle left the elevators at the ground floor and hurried across Thompson Street, turned left, and jogged as far as Bleecker Street, where it turned left again and descended a small set of stairs into a nondescript student bar. If she had hurried in after it, Anouk would have arrived in time to see the ankle's owner cross the bar and enter a door to the right of the kitchen, which, if she had still followed, would have led her down a hallway pinned by fluorescent lights and through another door at the other end, which opened into a dim room furnished only with oversized cushions. The room was already filled with a number of people sitting on the cushions and drinking wine. And, eyes slowly adjusting to the darkened room after the hard, bright hallway, Anouk would have witnessed the people in the room appearing to play a game of marbles. Their cushions were arranged in a vague circle, and on the floor in the center was a small pile of smooth, round jacks and moons and spiders. As the Pink Tracksuit entered, a story was in progress. "I knew I was lost, and I could hear the footsteps keeping pace with mine," a voice said breathlessly from somewhere in the room, while everybody laughed and cheered and talked over the storyteller. But when they saw the Pink Tracksuit, the room fell silent except for the storyteller, who, from an unidentified corner continued, "I felt a hand on my shoulder and tried to scream …" Then somebody gathered up the marbles and dropped them into a cloth bag. The storyteller stopped, and all eyes turned to the Pink Tracksuit.

"She was awake again," the Pink Tracksuit told them. "That damned girl never sleeps."

"You're gonna lose," said another, "You should find somebody else."

The Pink Tracksuit smirked. "You know you got nothin' on my girl when she comes through. Ooh, you'll look so sweet in your mama's lilac dress, Danny-boy. I can't wait to see it."

Everybody laughed. Dan said, "Don't talk too soon. The bet's not going your way so far," but few people heard over the chatter that restarted. People cast more marbles into the center of the room, and a new storyteller began a tale. "The night my father hit my mother for the third time was the night before the day I won the debating prize for the whole county …"

The Pink Tracksuit joined the rest of the group on the cushions.

CHAPTER 4

At 10:00 on Monday morning, now fully recovered from the hangover he suffered the day before, the old man put down *Gone Fishin'*, shuffled into the kitchen, flipped the kettle on, and lit a cigarette while he waited for the kettle to boil.

At noon, freshly showered, he made himself a salami and ketchup sandwich and indulged in two gingersnap cookies.

At 2:30 PM, in Salem, a beautiful, overly made-up woman returned from the dead once again, this time having received plastic surgery on a deserted island and looking nothing like her former self, to reclaim her lost love who had unfortunately moved on and was embroiled in a passionate affair with the woman's twin sister, who looked exactly the way her sister used to look *before* the surgery, and who may or may not have been hatching a twisted, evil plan.

At 4:00 PM, the old man checked the mailbox. Nothing.

Airmail

No telephone calls, either.

On Tuesday at 11:30 AM, management in the old man's building arranged for the lawns to be mowed. The cut grass smelled good, and he opened the lounge room windows.

By 2:00 PM, he started to sneeze, and his eyes were red and swollen, so he got up and shut the windows again. When *Days of Our Lives* finished, he walked to the local chemist to buy hay fever medicine. It was 4:15 PM when he returned, well past post time, so he checked the box. Nothing.

On Wednesday, he took the trash out at 9:00 AM while still in his dressing gown in case he forgot it later in the afternoon.

The post was late. The old man checked it at 4:05 PM out of habit, even though there had been no sound or scent of two-stroke. Then he checked it again at 4:25 PM as the mailman scootered away up the hill. Empty.

On Thursday at noon, the old man ran out of ketchup. Instead, he had English mustard with the salami on his sandwich.

The woman in Salem was devastated at her lover's betrayal. At 3:20 PM, she vowed in tears and soft focus to exact her revenge on both her lost love and her evil twin.

Four o'clock in the afternoon was post time. There was a letter addressed to Mr. G. L. Solomon, sent with a U.S. stamp. It was from the stranger. He took the letter inside, reached into the shoebox under the green trim of the armchair, and placed the letter in the box, unopened, on top of the other letters.

The woman in the portrait on the wall watched, puzzled. He did this every time. Why didn't he open the letter straight away? She could tell he was curious. The portrait had never understood the old man, even when the old man was a young man.

The old man slowly traced his fingers over the small video library on the bottom shelf in his lounge room and pulled out *The Great Escape*. He settled back on the chair to watch, and the portrait could almost see him consciously *not* thinking about the letter in the box underneath.

* * *

At 9:00 the following morning, fully dressed, the old man poured himself a glass of whiskey, no ice. He took the letter out of its box under the armchair, settled back, took a big sip of the whiskey, and opened it. His hand was shaking, but that could well have been age, not to mention the early hour for drinking. From her place on the wallpaper, the portrait held her breath.

The letter smelled mildly of dairy. Sweet and bacterial. The paper was thick, and there were greasy, thumbprint smudges along the edges, and something that could possibly have been cat hair. The old man screwed up his nose momentarily and then started to read.

> Dear G. L.,
>
> I can't sleep. I wonder if you ever have that trouble. It's possible it's a guilty conscience that's stopping me—that's what they say in the movies ...

The old man read the letter exactly twice. Then he drained the last of his now-warm whiskey, put the letter and the matches in the shoebox under the armchair, took the whiskey glass to the sink, and flipped the kettle on. He lit a cigarette while he waited for the kettle to boil and got a china teacup and tea bag ready, leaving the saucer in the cupboard. It was 10:00 AM.

*　*　*

At that moment, being also exactly 6:00 the night before, at Houston on Broadway, Manhattan, New York, United States of America, Earth, Anouk ran across the road. For her life.

But she was not running away from anything. She appeared to chase a short, chubby, black woman who was wearing a pink velour tracksuit, and wherever the woman dodged along the streets heading north up Broadway, Anouk followed. The woman dashed into side alleys and hid in doorways, and Anouk followed. The woman darted out and then rushed back to Broadway to try to hide herself in the crowds, but Anouk had trained her eyes on the pink backside as it wobbled and sweated, and she kept chasing.

The Pink Tracksuit did not appear to run in fear; her eyes were strangely exultant. But Anouk wore the face of a hunted animal as she chased because she knew the woman who was running away ran with her life. The Pink Tracksuit, whose palms were now shiny with sweat, kept a tight grasp on a biscuit tin that rattled when she ran. It was the contents of this tin that held the answer to whether or not Anouk would live through the night.

Ever-busy New Yorkers yelled angrily at Anouk as she rushed after the tracksuit, breathing heavily. She wove through the market stalls now, tripping over the flimsy outdoor tables containing I Heart NY T-shirts, mesh slippers, hats, and replica packs of playing cards containing Islamic human targets in the guise of hostile soldiers.

Ahead of her, the woman in the pink tracksuit caused a lot less trouble, weaving her fat bottom in between crowds of shoppers and vendors and office workers without eliciting any of the angry yells that built up in Anouk's wake.

Sometimes, the woman looked back to see if Anouk still followed. She smiled as if the chase were a game to her. The contents of the tin rattled.

They kept running. For a chubby, sweaty person, the Pink Tracksuit was in great shape. Anouk could see the Flatiron building growing closer; they had run for several miles. The crowds were worse up here. Taxis clogged the roads, and human ants swarmed in and out of the subway holes as eight million people started their journeys home from work. Pink Tracksuit ran through the crowds, seemingly without effort, a good block ahead now but still in sight.

Then, without warning, the woman tripped. A false move. And as she fell, the tin box sailed into the air, curving backward and creating an arc over the heads of the crowd. It broke open on the footpath a few yards behind.

Through the crowds, Anouk could not see the contents of the tin spilling out and over the pavement, tossed and kicked under thousands of feet, some tumbling into drains and over onto the road beneath the wheels of the taxis. But she felt them spill from somewhere inside her, and she abruptly stopped running. She sat down, feeling a burning sensation in her chest, and in a shrill whistle, her air escaped.

CHAPTER 5

The letter was dated two weeks earlier. The memento in the envelope this time, if you could call it a memento, was a used sheet of foil packaging that had once contained ten individual doses of Ambien.

>Dear Mr. G. L.,
>
>Joseph has brought me sleeping tablets—the kind you can only get with a prescription. I don't know how he got them, because as far as I know, he's never had a problem sleeping in his life, but I guess in this town, prescription drugs are pretty easy to get. I told Joseph I was fine and would sleep soon and wouldn't need the drugs, but he said they were for him, not me, and that he needed me to sleep because apparently I am intolerable. Joseph tells me I snap at people with no cause, fail to pay attention

to important conversations, am rude to waiters, and prone to spontaneous bursts of nonsense. I, of course, do not recall any of this behavior and suspect he is overreacting because he is becoming hypersensitive that I still do not wish to discuss his latest philosophy paper, 'The Contemporary Bourgeois: *Melrose Place* and Plato's Simulacrum.' This is because I do not understand a word of it. Some guff about nothing being as it seems and a puppet show. I can tell this to you, G. L., but I need to keep Joseph thinking that he and I are on the same page. So the sleeping pills have sat in my little room for just under a week now. At night, I lie in a half dream but still awake state, and it gets bloody tempting to use them. I mean, nobody enjoys insomnia. It's just that something in me is afraid to surrender myself to being truly, vulnerably asleep. And maybe to not wake up for hours. Which, come to think of it, may be the reason why I do not sleep at all. Thank you, G. L.; you may have helped me hit on something!

Here, the ink color changed from black to blue.

I still have not slept. And I am still being followed, though this has become so much of my daily (and nightly) experience that I have to concentrate now to single out the moments. The Pink Tracksuit is a lot less subtle these days. I actually see her spying on me, peering from behind street poles, for example. I see the profile of her nose and one eye squinting, watching me; she thinks she's hidden, but apart from the suggestion of her face, there's a whole acre of velour-clad ass waggling repulsively out the other end of the pole. Honestly, she has no idea. It would be funny if it wasn't so scary. Each night, at odd hours, I hear footsteps or scratching at my door. Sometimes I sit awake with the lights turned out, watching this city from my window pass and play through all the dark hours—eight million insomniacs. A couple of times, I've heard noises in the hallway, looked, seen the shadow of footsteps pause at my door, seen them pass, return, and pause again. Once, the doorknob turned, toppling the marble I had carefully balanced on it (with great difficulty, I can tell you). It clattered to the floor and sent the footsteps in a thumping flurry down the hallway, not to return that night. I want to sleep, but often I think it is being awake that saves me from whatever it is she plans. You know those kids' books, *Where's Wally?* Here in the States, they call Wally "Waldo." I don't know why. But now, going out in the daytime is like a *Where's Wally/Waldo* adventure to find the Pink Tracksuit in the crowd. She hides, but she hardly blends, and I see her everywhere.

I think I will take one of Joseph's sleeping tablets, after all.

Anouk

CHAPTER 6

Another two weeks passed by without new mail, although the Thai takeout restaurants appeared to have embarked on a frenzied marketing competition centered around the old man's mailbox.

Mario handed over management of The Colonnade to Johnny, a Bosnian refugee with a piece of bullet permanently wedged in the side of his skull, who liked to play Elvis Presley loudly on the jukebox and sing along. The old man, therefore, spent the next pension week Saturday afternoon boozily singing "Love Me Tender" in a less than musical tenor, arm in arm with Mario, Ciro, and Tony.

When evening fell, they all moved upstairs for spaghetti, wine, and illegal gambling. Drunk, broke, and happy, the old man made his way home on the last bus.

In the lounge room late that night, the portrait almost smiled as the old man stumbled into his bedroom, pajama bottoms askew.

* * *

By Monday, the old man had recovered from his hangover, and at 4:00 PM, there was a letter in the mail. And according to his now familiar ritual, he put it aside. At 9:00 AM on Tuesday, with a glass of whiskey at hand, he opened it, and when he finished reading, he carefully folded it up and placed it on the sideboard. He poured another whiskey, returned to the sideboard, and unfolded the letter again. It trembled in his hand.

Dear Mr. G. L., I am writing to you from the Other Side, it began. He put the letter down, took another big slurp of the whiskey, and picked it back up.

> Dear Mr. G. L.,
>
> I am writing to you from the Other Side. It's not what I expected, the world of the dead—not that different from New York, really. I still watch crowds of strangers from my window, and I still can't sleep at night. There are cats here, too.
>
> Joseph takes the ferry across the river Styx to visit me, his face appearing out of the afternoon (here, it is always afternoon) full of philosophy and concern, but he no longer speaks English—or perhaps I now only understand the language of the dead. His speech is garbled, and he leaves me frustrated each afternoon (I'm frustrated, that is; I can't speak for Joseph).
>
> Mainly, though, it's boring. There's only Joseph's sideburned face to break the monotony; none of

my other friends come. I find I even miss the Pink Tracksuit, my constant companion for many months. I don't have a job, and there is nowhere to go. There is just my mattress and paper, paper, paper on which to write. To you, to myself. Who will read what I write?

Thinking about it, I don't know why I wrote to you when I was alive. Maybe, I just wanted to be real. I escaped everything in Sydney, left the country, and changed my name. No trail to my life and sadness and failure and reality. And him. And only you, a stranger, G. L., to know that I live and exist, reading letters written by my own hand and signed with my real name.

And that is ironic, given that now I am writing to you while I am dead. If proof of existence was my motive, why do I still write now that I no longer exist?

I find myself wondering for the first time what you might be thinking when you open my mail. What is your response to these uninvited letters from a stranger? What do you do when you read them? Are you reading them? What is your name? Are you alone or surrounded by a wife and a mistress and seven children? Or are you young and brave? And do you enjoy a really good party?

Perhaps, now that I am dead, you will come alive in my head.

Something has just occurred to me: I don't know where to get stamps. How will you receive my letter? Maybe there are thousands, or millions, of dead people all writing letters to their loved ones—or to strangers—that they can never send because there are no stamps in Hades.

I have no leftovers from cafés or bars or restaurants to include for you this time—only the charcoal that still tumbles from my hollow insides when I cough. Perhaps it is a piece of femur, but then again, I may be sending you a piece of my heart. I do not recommend internal combustion as a way to go.

Yours,

Anouk

The old man refolded the letter and slipped it back into the envelope, which was lined with fine, gray ash. As he placed it in the shoebox under the armchair, his hand shook violently, and it took three attempts to fit the lid back on the box. The second glass of whiskey was long since empty.

For the first time in what was probably decades, he looked up at the old portrait of the young woman. "Quiet, you," he said to her unblinking eyes.

He flipped on the kettle and lit a cigarette, but when the kettle boiled, he smoked a second cigarette instead of making the tea.

Then, without getting changed or even shaving, he took the 380 bus to the city and went straight to Stanley Street, the first time in twenty years he had done so outside of a Saturday.

The men were already there, drinking, smoking, laughing, and gambling just as if it was pension week Saturday every day. "Prego!" Mario yelled, as usual, and he poured the old man a prelunch grappa.

The old man woke late the next morning, the beginnings of a gray beard bristling on his cheeks, and the beginnings of a hangover headache ringing in his ears. He shuffled in his slippers to the lounge room sideboard and poured a glass of whiskey.

Feeling better, the old man showered and shaved, dressed in his permanent crease pants, and was at Stanley Street again by midday. He joined the other men at the café tables in front of The Colonnade and drank three short blacks in quick succession, courtesy of Mario. Together, they watched the day, flirted with the young women for all the world as if they had a chance, and exchanged nods with the young men. For five days, the old man eschewed his old routine and embraced a new one. Old man gossip, cigarettes and cigars, home brew everything alcoholic, endless pasta, Julia's vanilla gelato, and consistent losses at the cards. Hangovers every morning.

The old man chain-smoked cigars to rid his fingers of the scent and stain of the stranger's ash.

* * *

On Monday at 11:00 AM, the old man walked to the shops to buy three things: more Tylenol, a guidebook to New York, and the most detailed map of Manhattan he could find in the bookstore.

By 12:30 PM, he was back home. He took the shoebox out from under the armchair and carried it to the kitchen. He spread the map on the table, pushing the remnants of his lunch to the side. One by one, he took out the stranger's letters and marked each area or landmark she mentioned in thick, red marker. SoHo, NoHo, Upper West Side, Broadway and Houston, East Village, Chelsea. In the guidebook, he looked up the locations of Flatiron, La Esquina, Magnolia, and Yankee Stadium.

He looked in vain for a necropolis.

* * *

Joseph, however, traversed the New York City of the dead twice daily to visit Anouk. It could be found downtown on Thompson Street, and it bore a remarkable resemblance to Anouk's old boardinghouse, although certain things had changed. Inside, for example, the television was resolutely quiet. The cats were gone. The little kitchenette gathered dust, although there were half-eaten boxes of Chinese takeout in various stages of decomposition scattered around the floor and foldout bed. On the bed, Anouk sat and wrote. Sometimes letters to G. L., sometimes letters to herself, sometimes letters to an unnamed lover.

On the day that Anouk ran out of paper on which to write, she began scribbling on the walls. She wrote long epistles to Mr. G. L. about life in Hades, cursive stretching the breadth of the little room. By the time Joseph made his evening visit, she had almost covered an entire wall.

He pulled the permanent marker from her hand and gently guided her back to the bed, pushing aside the food boxes, which he would clean up later. He cradled Anouk's head on his shoulder and rocked slowly, telling her stories about his day and his studies and his latest discoveries. Anouk ignored Joseph, refusing to acknowledge his presence, but she relaxed against his body and didn't try to move away.

Later, while Anouk slept and Joseph attempted to clean the room, he saw that she had written in the permanent marker on the dirty gray blanket of her bed, "Joseph." Elsewhere on the blanket, she had written, "Joseph crosses the river Styx. Don't pay the ferryman."

The next day, he bought her a thick book of writing paper. She took the gift without acknowledging the giver and immediately began writing.

> Dear Mr. G. L.,
>
> Does there occur a moment in time that acts like suction, pulling and drawing all that was once destructive and unresolved in a life into the broken mind to fill and flood and overwhelm? And if yes, what happens to the stories? Can he, floating at the top of the debris, destroy me?

CHAPTER 7

There was a letter in the box.

The old man returned to his routine, as suddenly absent from Stanley Street outside of pension week Saturdays as his appearance had been that unusual Tuesday, but the Italian Old Guard of his day fourteen revelries was unperturbed. Here was wine and Julia's unsurpassable gelato.

The letter consisted of just one line: "Joseph does not know my real name. He thinks it is R———."

CHAPTER 8

Three weeks passed. At 4:05 PM every weekday, the old man checked the mailbox, but it remained empty apart from real estate ads, even when he felt inside to be sure. The fat tabby knew the old man's shuffle and kept out of sight in the afternoon.

This week's sandwiches were lettuce, tuna, and mayonnaise, prepared at precisely noon to be eaten at 12:15 PM at the kitchen table. The old man no longer looked at the red-marked map that gathered dust at the other end of the table.

Fishing World was road testing a new type of sinker with a shifting weight inside that caused the bait to jerk and sway slightly of its own accord. A thin woman from Castle Hill named Rowena was up to $200,000 on *Who Wants to be a Millionaire?* Troops were withdrawing from Iraq. A toddler was inadvertently kidnapped when a teenager stole a car, not realizing that the child was asleep in the back. The Salem lovers were back together and about to renew their wedding vows, but the jilted twin planned mischief.

The following week was salami and ketchup for lunch. The mailbox remained empty each day. The telephone never rang.

On Thursday, the old man gathered the junk mail together and tossed it into the recycle bin. As the bright paper fluttered down, one caught his eye. It was a red and white card, and when he picked it up, he saw it was a parcel notice from the post office addressed to Mr. G. L. Solomon. He had almost missed it among the green-grocer calendar cards and pizza delivery special offers. The checkbox ticked said "normal parcel."

Without stopping to lock the unit, the old man shuffled straight to the post office before it closed. He still wore his house slippers.

* * *

At 5:15 PM, the parcel sat on the kitchen table. It was addressed to Mr. G. L. Solomon and carried U.S. stamps, but the handwriting was unfamiliar. He watched the unopened parcel while he smoked a cigarette and waited for the kettle to boil, routine once again gone to seed.

He opened the parcel. There was a typewritten note, dated last month, resting on top of a large, square tin.

"Your lady friend isn't dead. I thought to write you from this letter I found in her pockets. Here is what's left of her stories. Most were lost. Now play."

There was no signature on the note.

Craning to read the words, the portrait on the wall thought the tone was vaguely malicious. She didn't trust it. And the challenge, "Now play," put the portrait in mind of unknown danger. But the old man asked no questions of the portrait's faded eyes. He was intent on the package.

Airmail

The tin was Australian—Arnotts—and inside it when the old man lifted the lid were three marbles and a letter in the stranger's scrawling handwriting. He opened the letter first.

Dear Mr. G. L.,

I could have been wrong about the thriller movie search for answers. I don't think she's from this world at all. Of course I mean the Pink Tracksuit. I think she wants something worth more than money. She wants my stories. And I know how she appears in front of me wherever I am—she is writing herself into this story as she goes.

You probably think I'm crazy or had too many nights of insomnia, and it may be true, but think about it—all the coincidences that happen in life, the unexpected meetings, and the "six degrees of separation" weirdness—I mean, it really works. I've tried it. There is a maximum of six people between us and any other person on the planet. Probably you and I could link up with even fewer. So maybe, just maybe, all this ties together because someone is writing us this way like a giant, universal Dickens.

And what if Dickens wasn't the only storyteller? What if there were more? And what if they competed with each other like the ancient gods of Olympus? What if the storytellers were consumed with writing the most profound tales, collecting the best stories, and influencing the greatest adventures like children on the street competing for the most rare and valuable marbles?

What if I am trapped in a Pink Tracksuit story partly of her making, and partly because she wants what I have lived and collected so far?

And what if? What if she steals my stories for a game? What if it's as simple as that and as random and complex and chaotic as the meaning of the universe? What then? What am I?

The old man turned the letter over, but the rest of it was blank. He looked at the three marbles and then looked more closely. There was nothing remarkable about them. Three simple jacks in various colors.

He picked one up. It was warm to touch.

THE FIRST MARBLE

The Good Little Girl

My name is Anouk. When I was little, I had every intention of being a very good little girl. But apparently, I kept doing things that were bad.

This is the first story that I remember. We were visiting the house of two little girls, and the eldest had a serious temper. When it was time for me to go home, she grew upset because our games had been such fun. First she cried, and then she picked up her toys and threw them about the room. Then she kicked the cupboards and kicked her mother and cried some more. I watched, thinking what a very naughty girl she was, having suffered the raw side of my mother's hand on more than one similar occasion. Her mother chastised her angrily, and, in the heat of the mother's tirade, the little girl stormed off into her room and slammed the door behind her.

I was astonished. This was the best good little girl I had ever seen. Fancy knowing that she was about to be sent to her room and taking herself there without being told. And doing it all with such energy and before she had recovered enough to be sorry. This was a forward thinking, obedient little person, even in the midst of a temper, and I was very impressed.

I don't remember why I had my own next tantrum, or even having it, but I do recall my mother speaking angrily at me, and I recall the exact moment at which I remembered the good little girl and decided to impress my mother by trying the same trick. So, midway through my mother's furious speech, I left her and positively ran to my room, slamming the door behind me with gusto and waiting for the inevitable loving praise that would follow.

I didn't have to wait long. The door swung open and there was my mother, wooden spoon in hand.

The Dirty Little Girl

I remember my first day at school, and it was a bitter disappointment. This was a day I had anticipated for years. Every morning, I would sit on the wide windowsill of our family room and watch the big kids walk to school dressed in their blue plaid uniforms with bags on their backs and wish I was one of them. I begged my parents to teach me to read, but they had strange theories about encouraging me to play and enjoy life, telling me silly things like there being plenty of time for me to read and write the rest of my life.

So on the first day of school, while all the other children were crying and clinging to their mothers and begging them not to go, I was embarrassed that my mother was still around. She was getting in the way of learning. Calmly, I advised her that she was free to go home now, which she did, head hanging.

Then I entered my classroom, sat down, and waited for the learning to begin. The first thing I discovered was that we were going to spend the next two weeks playing games, tying oversized shoelaces on a cardboard sneaker on the wall, and getting to know one another. I realized by play-lunch that I was not going to return home this afternoon able to read books or solve mathematical problems.

The second great disappointment was Chadwick Bevan. Chadwick's parents had taught him to read as a little baby, and by the age of three, he was reading the newspaper. Now he was on to grown-up books. I was mortified. Chadwick Bevan had been given a head start, and my parents had, by insisting that I play, forever ruined my chances of being the smartest in the class.

In the afternoon, sitting in a circle with our teacher, we were challenged to hide a brightly colored, plastic building block somewhere on our person, and each of us was to guess where the others had hidden their blocks. Determined at least to shine in this task, I slipped my block into the seat of my bloomers and waited.

I definitely won that game; the other children could not guess where my block was hidden, not even when they got up from the circle and walked around me. But when I triumphantly displayed my clever hiding place, our teacher was less than impressed. It transpired that I was, in fact, a dirty little girl. The teacher was so angry that she sent me to tell Mrs. Yale what I had done.

Mrs. Yale was the other kindergarten teacher, and had, on day one, already managed to instill fear into all our hearts. She was an ogre, and this was not a metaphor; she had the facial warts to prove it. I crept into the room where the ogre was reading to her class on the floor and waited for my courage to rise to the occasion. It was a little slow coming, and the story was mildly interesting, so in the interim, I sat down at the back of the group to listen.

The story was about Ping, a little duck that lived on a boat in China with a lot of other ducks and one master. Every evening, the master would call the ducks in from the lake to shelter on the boat, and the last one to waddle up the ramp and onto the deck would get a whack with a stick. One evening, Ping was a long way from the boat, and he knew he would be last and didn't want to get whacked with the stick. So instead of swimming to the boat, he hid in the long reeds. The boat went on without him, and Ping had lots of adventures, most of them unpleasant. Then one evening, after he had almost died from cold and cruel hunters, he saw the boat again, quite some distance away. The master was calling the ducks and he knew he'd be last in, but he swam for the boat, anyway. Sure enough, the master whacked Ping with the stick, but he didn't care. He was happy to be home.

I found the story greatly disturbing and became fully engrossed. That is where my own teacher found me when the bell rang to go home, and nothing more was said of the blocks.

CHAPTER 9

The old man dropped the marble back into the tin as though it burned his palm, and the story stopped, leaving five-year-old Anouk alone in kindergarten with her books and blocks.

He looked at the clock on the wall. It was 10:13 PM, but he wasn't ready to sleep. He turned on the television and watched the end of a detective drama and then the *Late News* without taking any of it in.

The old man's hands were not shaking now, not one bit, and he was surprisingly full of energy. He stood up, and he sat down. He stood up and walked to the kitchen door, where he paused for no good reason, while the *Late News* rolled on without knowing or caring that an elderly recluse was currently undergoing an existential crisis. At a loss, he sat back down again and watched the television without seeing the television.

But in his mind's eye, the old man saw Anouk as though he had known her all his life. She had pale olive skin that would brown quickly in the sun and give her a Mediterranean appearance. At three, her dark hair was long and tangled with curls. By the time she started school, it was cropped into neat, shoulder-length domesticity and had thickened. Despite her olive skin, she had very rosy cheeks. She frowned a lot, two little lines bisecting her eyebrows that would trouble her when she grew older, and her lower lip frequently protruded in a pout.

The lines on the old man's face softened.

It was late, and the television played failed American sitcoms. He did not know what to do. There was no routine to explain airmail letters from a stranger, coughed-up charcoal from a femur or heart, a biscuit tin from the Pink Tracksuit, six degrees of separation, and a marble that contained a little girl.

The old man took out a notebook and a ballpoint pen and carefully wrote the following:

"Was Dickens a god?"

"Was Plato a puppet?"

"What is the meaning of life?"

The old man put the pen down and then picked it up again and added to the list:

"Who is Joseph?"

At 2:38 AM, the old man picked up the same marble; it was warm.

>My name is Anouk. When I was little, I had every intention of being a very good little girl. But apparently, I kept doing things that were bad.

Her story was still alive.

At 3:59 AM, the old man fell asleep in the green armchair.

* * *

When he woke in the morning, sore and old, the old man showered, shaved, and put on his front-creased pants and best shirt. He put on a tie and then thought better of it and took it off. He poured a half-glass of whiskey, took a sip, and then he tipped the rest down the sink. He poured full cream milk over two cups of cooked oatmeal and stoically ate the lot. He flipped on the kettle and made a cup of tea without using a saucer.

He emptied the shoebox of letters and put them all in the biscuit tin over the marbles, with the typewritten note from the Pink Tracksuit on the top. He took the neglected map of New York, already covered in red marks and lines, and wiped the dust and dinner splashes from its surface. He lit a cigarette and mused over the map while he smoked. When he finished the cigarette, he ashed it, emptied the tray, and washed the tray up. Then he carefully dried his hands on a clean tea towel and folded the map until it was small enough to fit in the biscuit tin. The old man put the lid on and left the tin on the kitchen table.

In his bedroom, he opened the cupboard doors. He pulled out his second-best pair of permanent-pressed trousers and two pairs of the soft, cotton pants he normally wore about the house, carefully folded them, and placed them on the bed. He did the same with exactly five collared, short-sleeved shirts. When the old man finished preparing his clothes, he dragged a dusty sports bag from the bottom of the closet and filled it.

Airmail

The crooked portrait on the wallpaper remembered that, in the 1970s, during one of the old man's other lives, this bag had held tennis racquets and balls and shoes and a change of clothes and possibly a book or magazine to read later, alone, in the clubhouse.

From the second drawer in his bathroom, he took an unopened packet of twelve disposable razors, a half-used can of aftershave, and other assorted toiletries. These went into the sports bag loose because there were no other bags.

Then he closed the zipper.

He went into the kitchen, picked up the biscuit tin, reopened the bag, and placed the tin inside, closing the zipper. He changed his mind, pulled the tin out, and rested it carefully on top of the bag.

The old man placed everything sitting ready in his lounge room and left it behind to walk to the shops. He visited the bank and removed all his savings. This took some time, as the old man was required to provide more identification than he held with him, and he had to return to the house to retrieve legitimate proof of his existence. After he finished at the bank, he visited the student discount travel agent and asked for the first plane to New York City.

The first seat available would be ready in one week. The old man had not been prepared for this.

He returned home but did not unpack the bag. Instead, he lived in his one spare pair of pants, two shirts alternating each day, and underwear rinsed out each night and left to dry for the morning. The razor that had already been in use and so left out of the packing had to serve him all week, as did the half-finished soap for cleaning his hair as well as his body. The old man refused to open the bag; it sat beside the green armchair, ready for a journey.

The old man had a passport, which he had diligently renewed every ten years since 1964. There were no stamps inside it.

On the sixth day, the evening before he was due to leave, the old man opened the biscuit tin. He removed the typewritten note and the letters, and he reached for one of the marbles on the bottom. Like the other, it felt warm.

THE SECOND MARBLE
Fabio

My name is Anouk, and when I was nineteen, I was in a foreign country looking for a doctor to abort the child I was carrying by a foreign man I did not love. This is how it happened.

I was writing in my journal at the outdoor tables of a gelateria in Rome, far from any of the main attractions but never far, in this city, from history.

"Hello," said a voice to my left as I turned the page of my journal. The man spoke in English with a French accent. He was very handsome, with long, blond hair, longer and softer than mine, and a hard, brown body that even under the tailored T-shirt said *workout*. I was nineteen, you will recall, and he was very attractive, so I stayed for more gelati and espresso. I spoke a little French, and he spoke a lot of English and enough Italian to get us by.

The weeks that followed had a lot less to do with Rome than with Fabio (his real name was Raoul, but I called him Fabio because I could not believe it was not butter). We spent our days seeking private places in public hostels and stealing embraces in cupboards. I started to lose my suntan.

After a month, my visitor's visa ran out, and it was time for me to return to my Round the World ticket, so I left Fabio and Rome for London. I missed his embraces but was pleased to resume my adventure. After all, I was here to see new things. Men were not new; men were everywhere, even at home.

I joined a party of my friends who were already in London. Together, we were unabashed tourists. We traced around all the pubs on the grubby Monopoly Board path, leaving a trail of drunken Australians behind as our group dwindled, scandalizing Park Lane and Mayfair with our antics.

I was eating and drinking so much that I failed to notice anything unusual about the swelling in my belly. I left my friends in London and bounced back alone to Zurich for some cheese.

This was where I realized, gradually, that I no longer bled.

I had an appointment within two weeks, and I will not speak of that process except to reassure that it did not hurt where I expected. But elsewhere, there was a great and unexpected tearing that ached as much with surprise as blood, and there was no anesthetist to numb the sensation.

I believe I am the mother of a little girl. I guess her hair would be soft and light and her skin brown. At nineteen, I had not learned to love, but nor had my heart learned to shrink in pain.

My little child did not learn these things, either.

Fabio's Legacy

My French lover left me something else beyond a child that didn't exist—something that would be with me forever.

A few weeks after I rescued my little girl from the hardening of her heart, I felt a burning where I should not, and when I was almost unable to walk, I returned to the doctor who had helped me so recently. She took tests that made me scream and cry, my body clinging to its precious infection. In agony and sickness, I spent a week in bed.

It was punishment, I believed at the time, for deserting my child.

Instead, it was revealed to be no more than punishment for being less than careful with a traveler met in Rome who bore more than a passing resemblance to the cover of too many bodice-ripping romance novels. He left me sores that slowly healed, and a secret sickness that taught me what it felt like to be undesirable.

The doctor was practical and faced the world with less melodrama (and presumably less pain in her nether regions) than I. She assured me that my infection, once healed, would not transfer. I was free to be a desirable person, if I so chose. And I did.

But even today, if I feel anxious or weary or sick, the painful reminder of Fabio reappears, and I remember what he gave me. I remember what he will never know I rejected. So I will never forget, because even if my heart constricts to the size and chill of a glass marble, my body will remind me of what I have done.

Sleep Like a Child

When I was twenty, I returned to my parents' home and slept for a month. Exactly a month. I went to bed on the Anzac Day holiday, April 25. I slept as soundly as a child, and when I woke up on the afternoon of May 24, the weather had changed. There was a chill in the air that reminded me of Europe only a month and a day before, and I cried.

While I slept, my mind stopped, but everything else sped with health. My hair grew so long that my mother had to rebraid it every morning, and soon she had to place a washing basket at the side of my bed and coil the hair inside it to stop the cats from playing. My body grew strong, I gained the weight I'd dropped in my travels, and the blush my cheeks had lost gently returned.

The sleep was dreamless and beautiful, and it is no wonder that when I woke, I cried, because all my reality rushed back into my chest.

But all the while I slept, my mother tells me I was curled in the fetal position.

CHAPTER 10

When Joseph thought about it that morning alone over coffee at Dante, he realized it had been almost exactly nine months since he and Anouk had been friends. The same amount of time as a human pregnancy. Joseph liked to make comparisons like that. He felt the universe spoke through coincidences and comparisons, so he always tried to listen.

Nine months ago, Joseph had taken over the same small table in the corner of the café near the wall that he was sitting at now, covering it with his own notes and philosophy texts borrowed from the university library while he tried to map out a plan for his next paper. He felt rather than saw Anouk first, and he looked up to see her looming over the table.

"C'nI'veyasuga?" she had asked in a thick accent. English, he thought she sounded, or Australian. And completely unintelligible. And, *oh*, before he could even wonder what on earth it was she had said, his mind confirmed his eyes: she was beautiful.

"Sorry, what?" said his lips before his mind and eyes had time to tell them to try to be more suave.

"I've got no sugar at my table. C'n I've yours?"

He handed her the small ceramic container of paper sugar sachets, and she took it with a smile and said, "Thanks," before returning to her table and sitting down with her back to him.

The girl emptied two sachets of sugar into her coffee and stirred without looking at the cup before she sipped deeply. Joseph watched her small back and her long, dark hair tangled in curls just past her shoulders. He wasn't really thinking about much, although whatever was in his mind was pleasurable when she spoke again. This time, though, it wasn't to him.

"Sweet fucking *Christ*!" she yelled to the back of the room, spitting her coffee back into the mug. This was New York, so nobody in the café even bothered to look around, but Joseph grinned. He knew exactly what she was talking about while he took another sip of his own insipid brew.

He went back to his notes for about half an hour, and this time he noticed the girl coming before she reached the table. "Thanks," she said again, and she handed him back the sugar container.

"Oh, sure, no problem," he said, and again he felt like a fool.

"You a writer?" she asked, eyeing his books and typewritten notes.

"Student," he said modestly, though he'd have preferred to have said, "Philosopher."

He kept expecting the girl to walk away, but she didn't. "Whatchya studying?"

"Right now, More's *Utopia*."

And to his surprise, the beautiful girl sat down opposite him at his table. "Interesting. Buy me any drink other than coffee—I'll let you tell me all about it," she challenged, and so he did.

She drank noisily, slurping the saccharine hot chocolate over her top lip, creating deliberate milk moustaches and gurgling while he told her all about Aristotle and Henry VIII and contemporary communism. Every now and then she'd frown, two small lines bisecting her brows, and say, "Hmm," in response to his words. Encouraged, Joseph kept talking. She was a good listener, though she didn't contribute much.

After about an hour, she said, "Thanks. See ya." She left Joseph to pack up his books alone and the waitress to clean up the girl's licked-clean pie plate and second (empty) mug of hot chocolate.

But two days later, she was there again. "Hi." She grinned and sat with him as if they were old friends. "What's on today?"

And slowly, they'd fallen into the habit of meeting almost every day at Dante to discuss Joseph's ideas. Joseph was always full of ideas, and his eyes gleamed and his nose pores sweated when he was particularly excited about one thing or another. At first, the girl had been coquettish with him like on the first day, but over time, she dropped the deliberately broad accent and the playful poses and just sat and listened. Sometimes she seemed distant and sad, and he'd wonder if he was boring her, and at other times, she'd startle him by thumping the table with her fist and yelling in agreement at one thing or another he'd said, so he knew she was taking it all in. It was good to have someone who wanted to listen to his ideas.

But try as he might, Joseph could not get the girl to share her own opinion. She was a philosopher in her own right, he could tell, though probably not educated that way. It was more than a month before she'd told him her name, hesitating and looking at the table when he'd asked, before muttering, "R⎯⎯."

Joseph still thought she was the most beautiful woman he had ever known, but he was no longer nervous in her company.

Subtly, the dynamics between them changed, and he didn't know now if he had been placed in the role of brother, father, mentor, or potential lover, though he did realize the decision wasn't up to him. He very much doubted he'd be her lover, so he gave it up. Slowly, the sexual tension created by his admiration and her behavior dissolved into their conversation, sweetening it but disappearing like brown sugar in coffee. Sometimes, in particularly pensive moments, she would touch her slender hand to his face, and he'd flinch away, aware of how he looked and feeling a kind of repulsion on her behalf. She never took these actions as rejection but would slip out of her mood in an instant and laugh at him.

If he asked her too many questions about her life back in Australia, or what she was doing in New York, she'd close up and grow angry. She was unhappy—that was clear even when she laughed—and frequently bitter, rude, and selfish. The girl had more than one lover on any given week, and on the rare occasions she did open up to Joseph, she loved to regale him with comic stories about one poor broken heart after another. She told him she wasn't sleeping, which went a little way to explaining her erratic and frequently abrasive moods, though Joseph thought she could have tried a little harder to be nice. But if he ventured to suggest this to her, she'd smile at him with her head on the side, cheeky and confident in her success. "Don't be cranky," she'd say. "Tell me about Jung. I'm sorry." And he would tell her about Jung, or whatever it was he was exploring at the time, and she listened and sometimes banged the table again and said, "Yes!" And though by now he knew this was a ruse to disguise the fact that she was lost, he loved her for making such a silly effort to please him, and so in turn, he pretended to still believe it.

And then there was the day she arrived at Dante as usual one hot morning and announced, "Buy me a coffee. I have a stalker."

CHAPTER 11

The old man strained forward in the narrow aisle seat, stretching across his neighbors to watch Sydney tilt and recede as the plane turned, found its flight path, and climbed. The aircraft rattled so much on takeoff, especially at the back where he sat, that one of his fellow passengers suggested they may all need to get out and push. The old man chuckled.

The previous week had passed in a flurry of inaction. The old man would boil the kettle and then drink a whiskey instead, pick up a periodical and read through several pages without remembering the content, select a heroic movie from his Steve McQueen video collection, and stand by the window facing the mailbox while the movie played out alone. *Days of Our Lives* went unwatched, the lovers and the evil twin left to bicker in the dark. The packed bags stayed beside the armchair in the lounge room, although he sporadically took the biscuit tin containing the letters and marbles out of the bag, returned it, and then took it out again. There was no mail.

On the third day of the Great Wait, the telephone rang. The sound came from the bedroom, and for a moment, the old man could not place what it was. Then he realized and shuffled quickly to the bedside table and picked up the receiver. His "Hello?" was husky and tremulous, the voice of an old man who had not had reason to speak for many days. His tickets were ready for him to pick them up, and the flight would depart at 3:45 PM in three days' time. The old man flipped on the kettle again, didn't make tea, poured a whiskey straight up, drank half, tipped the other half out, poured another half, and drank that, too. He lit a cigarette, smoked about a third of it, and then ashed the rest in the empty whiskey glass. He shuffled into the living room, picked up *Gone Fishin'*, put it back down, and shuffled back to the kitchen to rinse out the whiskey glass. He flipped the kettle back on, and while he waited for it to boil, he put a teabag in the cup, which he placed on a matching saucer. After he made the tea, he carried it back into the living room to drink while reading *Gone Fishin'*. The teacup rattled in the saucer, which shook in his hand, and the old man frowned. He rolled his eyes at the portrait. "Yes, Ingrid," he said, and he could not be sure, but he thought the portrait somehow disapproved. Then, on an afterthought, he looked back up at the portrait and said, simply, "Good-bye."

The portrait thought, *Good grief,* and she left him to it.

The next day at the student travel center, a young woman explained to the old man the intricacies of travel insurance and talked him through the process of taking an overseas journey. The old man's hands shook again as he took the tickets from her, but that could have been as much age as excitement.

Takeoff was delayed, but by 6:30 PM, with dusk just starting to settle and with all the lights in all the buildings visually cleansing the city, the old man felt the plane rattle. He watched

Airmail

Sydney tilt, and he pressed the small of his back into the cramped seat and smiled.

The hours passed without being watched. The substandard meals at strange times excited the old man's taste buds. When all the in-flight movies finished and the flight stewards forced the lights down, the other passengers were lulled to sleep in the dark tunnel of sky, but the old man stayed awake. He walked to the front of the plane, almost to first class, before someone politely turned him around. He walked away, around the back and the kitchens and bathrooms, and up the other aisle. He sat back down, seatbelt off despite the signs, to touch the danger. The old man liked the accents of the flight stewards and smiled when they were curt or rude. But he could have done with a cigarette.

Gone was the elderly recluse of the old man's tiny, routine-ridden home. The man on the plane, suave with the flight stewards and articulate with his fellow travelers, was, instead, the same man who emerged on Stanley Street on pension week Saturdays. But this was a Wednesday. Or was it Thursday? And when he arrived in New York, would it be Tuesday? The old man was dizzy with the possibilities and felt so alive he could have kissed a cat.

Time travelled. The other passengers started to stir, and those in the window seats lifted their blinds. There was a thin orange line of fire in the sky, piercing the night and lifting it into blue and pink. The old man strained forward; he had never seen anything so beautiful. "Now I understand why ancient people prayed to the dawn!" he told his puffy-eyed neighbor. The old man had not slept for twenty-four hours, but he felt a surge of energy. For the first time in seventy-three years, he was having an adventure.

The lights came back on in the cabin, and the stewards served another out-of-kilter meal. The passengers and cabin crew all charged on through the black and orange sky, thousands of miles receding under and behind them in a roar. The fire outside had faded almost to nothing—not the dawn but the sunset again. How strange and how magical. There was a movie showing on the monitors, but the old man got up and strolled to the door, pressing up and peering through the porthole window that felt icy on his nose. Underneath him was a network of lights, splayed out in circles and lines like a spider's web, increasing in satellite centers before trailing off and then gathering in a new place. Unknown cities.

At the San Francisco airport, at God knew what time, every food store sold clam chowder. The old man wandered, still not having slept and still wide awake, waiting for his connecting flight in two hours. He tried the clam chowder. It was terrible, and he loved it.

Everybody was much friendlier on the flight from San Francisco to New York. They smiled, they inquired over him, they simpered and made him know he was elderly and fragile and worthy of more respect than the other passengers. Somewhere over the hours of reddish brown hills, his head rattling against the cold window, the old man slept.

CHAPTER 12

When the plane landed at JFK airport, a trail of dried dribble traced the old man's chin, and it was dark yet again. The cab journey into SoHo took a long time—forty minutes—although he was assured by the driver that this was a good run. The old man did not watch the city flash by or breathe the air with the purpose of knowing that he was breathing in America. He failed to notice that the cab driver was a short, chubby, black woman, and that her collar, under the polyester overcoat, was pink velour. The sleep on the final flight had exhausted him, and uncertainty bred in the back of his mind, which he tried to muster the energy to dismiss.

The old man got out at a hostel recommended by the travel agents because of its proximity to the various bars and restaurants he had outlined in his travel plans. It was noisy. There were young people on the stairs, in the hallways, and at the reception, and they were talking, singing, kissing, laughing, drinking, and smoking, and the music was invasive. While the receptionist searched for his key, he watched one couple at the bottom of the stairs. The couple locked in an embrace that made the old man think of his youth. They pressed against each other and the wall, the boy with his hands inside the girl's skirt and lifting her closer to him by the buttocks while they kissed.

Then the receptionist handed him a key, and he carried his bag up and past the oblivious couple to room 23. The old man had asked for a room of his own, but there were only three private rooms in this hostel, none of which were available. Instead, he was sharing with one other—it was this or the dormitories that slept a dozen to each room. In the end, the old man was glad. Single rooms were expensive, and he had to make his meager savings last.

Inside, room 23 was empty; the other occupant was out for the night or perhaps carousing in the hallway. The old man placed his bag on the floor and opened it. Carefully, he dug through it and one by one laid all his toiletries out on the bed. He opened the bag of disposable razors first and lined the razors up. He selected some fresh underwear, found his pajama bottoms and nightshirt, and took these, a towel, the razor, shaving cream, soap, talcum powder, toothbrush, and toothpaste to one of the communal bathrooms at the end of the hall. He showered, dusted himself with talcum powder, and prepared to shave, despite the stubble that he knew would pester his cheeks and chin by morning. It was 10:30 PM New York time. In his home, it was tomorrow afternoon, and *Days of Our Lives* was about to start.

Back in the room, smooth of face, the old man climbed into the little bed and prepared to sleep, but sleep was not prepared for him. The thump of the music shook through the thin walls, as did the laughter of everyone on the stairs. His mind, too, spun with too many thoughts.

So the old man sat back up, reached under the bed for the biscuit tin, and took out the third marble. It was warm.

THE THIRD MARBLE
The Great Love

My name is Anouk, and this is the story of the end of my first life. It begins, as all these stories do, with a great love. I fell in love with a man who was handsome and kind and smart and loyal and funny. He was the perfect man, and he loved me. How he loved me. He said he was a better person because of me. He made promises. He promised to write me a song.

"Don't worry," he would say if I was too tired to make love, "we will be making love for the rest of our lives. Won't we?"

And I would say, "Yes."

He talked earnestly, and we laughed and made secret, silly plans to elope under the deliciously tacky Las Vegas lights, but then he had a new thought. "When I marry you, I want it to be somewhere special," and he named his favorite city. "Will we do that?"

And I said, "Yes."

One day, he became very ill. He was in a great fever and grew delirious, refusing to let his body rest until he had fixed all the doors and windows in the imaginary house he swore he was building. He would not let me leave his side, holding my wrist with the steel grip of a dying man if I tried to leave the bed, mumbling and pleading, "Don't leave me." Later, when he was well again, I told him of his visions. He said, "Maybe I was building a house for us. Do you think so?"

And I said, "Yes."

His work drew him overseas, and after a week, I followed. We met at the airport and stayed in each others' arms the whole taxi ride to the hotel.

"I missed you so much," he said over and again. "You cannot know how much I missed you. Did you miss me?"

And I said, "Yes."

That night, together in bed, he said, "I want to be like this forever. Can we be like this forever?"

And I said, "Yes." Then I turned my head to the side and cried while we made love.

He told me he loved me. He said that what made me different from all the women in all the world was that *he* loved *me*. He gave me his ring to wear. It was too big, and I kept losing it, but I kept finding it again.

How I loved him. I stopped sleeping at night because I preferred to lie awake and think of him. I smiled at his name. I grew up. I tried to make myself the person he believed I could be.

But because this is a true story and not a fairy tale, my beautiful man changed his mind. "We are not equipped," he told me "to withstand the circumstances in our lives." I did not understand. He said that he had told himself to stop loving me, and it had worked.

When I heard this, I felt combustion, and flames licked my internal organs.

I had said "yes" too many times, and his betrayal broke me. First, I sank very low. I lost weight. I lost motivation. My great love would call to me, now missing me, now distant, now declaring his love, and now rescinding it again. I grew angry with him, reproachful and crying.

It was smoking inside my head and tinder inside my heart.

The Scream

There was a scream building up in my stomach that could not be heard. I searched the Internet for a way to make everything stop. He was everywhere in my life, never leaving me in peace, keeping me near—sometimes loving me with his body and tender as our days together, and then he was cruel, accusing, and cold.

There were other men who wanted me, but I had said "yes" too many times to a man I trusted, and no one else could speak to my body or my heart. Instead, these men became my hurt. I had to release the scream, so here is what I did.

First, I had sex with all the men that could not speak to me, hard of body and rough of chin. Not once did I make love, but I fucked and was fucked by countless men. I became known at every bar and every nightclub in my city. I was a guaranteed good time. There were wild, passionate men; soft, tender men; dangerous, selfish men; and distracted, distant men. And every time I bent for them and they entered me, my stomach said "no," and my heart grew smaller.

Then, my hurt unresolved, I tried to consume women. I do not recall the face or the name of the first woman I touched, but her lips were sweet, and when I kissed her, to my surprise, I was not repulsed, but aroused. And when I asked her to leave, she did so, softly and silently.

I tried again with other girls. Soon, I was as popular with the women in all the bars and nightclubs in my city as I was with the men. But, just like the men, I wanted the women to disappear, lose their faces and their identities, just as I hoped to lose mine. My heart grew dry as I stretched for each new body.

My secret was that I cried at night. I cried for the beautiful man who had loved me and then changed his mind. I cried because I knew I would hurt and use as many faceless people as I could, and I knew I was unstoppable, and that soon my heart would grow small and hard and cold as glass, and fall out of place and pass through me, unnoticed, into the Sydney sewers.

I had said "yes" too many times. That is why I ran here to the busiest city in the world, to get lost, and say "no" to everything. I will befriend a boy named Joseph because he buys me drinks, and I will give him nothing in return. I have changed my name. I will not tell it because it is not real, and it does not matter. What I wanted to do was kill Anouk, not create something new.

But the failure that would not let me physically kill this body, though I abused it, will not let me kill this identity. I write to a stranger, a man's name found in the white pages through the flick and point method. And writing to him keeps me alive.

I do not want another love, but maybe my heart will soften. Perhaps I should get a cat.

CHAPTER 13

The old man was having fun; there was no denying it. His roommate, Karl, was an irrepressible, twenty-four-year-old journeyman of the world who hailed, originally, from East Berlin. Karl regaled the old man at night with stories of his travels around America—dabbling with vampire tales in Rhode Island, a romance in New Orleans, becoming lost in the tiny town of Whitesboro, Texas, "finding himself" in New Mexico, and a bar fight in Los Angeles.

By day, the old man sought adventures of his own. He joined the crowds at the top of the Empire State Building and stayed until closing. He rode the Circle Line to the Statue of Liberty with all the Russian tourists. He drank single-malt whiskey at bars in Tribeca filled with beautiful young things.

The old man booked tickets in the bleachers at the old Yankee Stadium before it closed forever and wondered where Anouk had sat, not so long ago.

He bought hot dogs with "the works" and warm beer in plastic cups. He watched families feed ducks in Central Park.

He crossed a busy road and angrily yelled, "I'm *walkin'* here!" at the oncoming traffic in his best attempt at a Brooklyn accent, a secret smile owning his face for five blocks afterward.

When the old man grew tired, he returned to room 23 at the top of the stairs, dragged the room's vinyl chair under the window, and watched the city pass by. One day, the old man pulled out his camera. He carefully dusted the lens, adjusted the settings, and even cleaned and oiled the leather strap, using olive oil gleaned from the hostel kitchen. The next afternoon, he leaned out of the window and started taking pictures of people as they walked underneath him. It was reportage, in its way, and the old man seemed to recover some instinct long rusted. In time, the photographs became his habit. He developed a collection: the tops of people's heads, their hats, the way their arms swung opposite to their legs as they strode or followed awkwardly on the same side, their hands resting quietly in a lover's, cradling a cell phone, or feeding an unseen mouth with hot dog or Krispy Kreme or fries.

Not once did his own hands shake as he held each person in his lens.

On Friday at 9:00 PM, seated on a lounge in a dim, quiet corner of a Nolita bar, a half-downed longneck also on the table beside him and an overweight woman dressed in pink sitting unseen in the booth next door, the old man sipped a gin martini and waited.

Karl returned from the bathroom and gave half of a small, fat pill to the old man, who swallowed it with a deep gulp of his drink.

Karl smiled at him, picked up the beer, and they both leaned back and laughed.

At 9:30 PM, the old man sat up abruptly as he watched the room recede in a rush. "Is this it?" he asked Karl, his eyes on the now-distant furniture.

"It is sudden, yes?" Karl agreed. "And it will end just as quickly. Relax and enjoy."

At 9:40 PM, the old man hunched over his chair watching the floor intently, the only piece of the room not moving away from him of its own volition. Karl returned to the lounge, this time with a big bottle of sparkling mineral water, and he poured a glass for the old man, splashing and spilling it slightly with unsteady hands. "Don't be afraid," Karl told the old man. "It will play tricks on your brain. Soak it in." The old man continued to watch the floor.

At 9:41 PM, the old man's hands shook. Karl pulled out a cell phone from his jacket pocket and brought up several photographs on the small screen, inserting the phone between the old man's eyes and the floor. "Look, here is my mother and my two nephews. This one is my old girlfriend, but we broke up when I left Berlin. Very nice, yes? This one is my father; I will tell you a story about him." The old man's eyes flickered over the photographs, and Karl began a story about his father's disappearance from the rural family home in East Germany in 1984 and his subsequent reappearance in 1990—a full inch taller, a copious head of hair covering his previously bald pate, and minus memory or conversation aside from talk of rock-fishing techniques. When Karl finished, the old man eagerly told him the story of *The Great Escape*, which Karl had never seen or even heard of, so the old man inserted his own name into

Steve McQueen's role as he excitedly recounted his bold escape from the Nazi war camp. The suffering, the camaraderie, the loneliness in isolation, the almost unbearable suspense, and the tearing motorcycle chase were all as real as the now still but vastly expanded room, and the old man truly lived that other life.

At 10:00 PM, Karl's friends arrived to find Karl and the old man still hunched forward in animated conversation. The old man stood shakily and embraced the friends. "Each one of you is my family," he told them tearfully.

At 11:00 PM, they all left the bar, the old man treading warily around the tables and still talking animatedly to anyone who would listen, telling stories of other people's lives that he adopted as his own. Further along the same street, they entered a new and crowded place where there was dancing, but after a few frenetic attempts, the old man conceded his age and era and instead became fascinated by the progress of his hands through the liquid air. His old legs were not tired, and his old heart was not taxed. He went to the bar and struck up a conversation with his neighbors to the left and right. "My name is G———. I have come here from Australia to find a young lady who may or may not be dead, though she writes me letters," he told them.

After this, there were many other nights like it. Karl took the old man to clubs and bars where chemicals created a new reality for the crowds, and the old man could slip in and out of each. "The Old Aussie" became a mascot for Karl and his friends—adored, indulged, and a mystery.

The old man's head was alive with new stories, and his shoes wore down from walking each day. At night, he dreamed of marbles, his own marbles copulating stories, feeding on one another, and multiplying like the magician's apprentice. They filled buckets, overflowed and rolled over tables, and shattered teacups and buried silverware in their deluge. They rose to the ankles, poured up, and spilled over furniture until he smothered inside his house, forced to breathe in warm, hard glass and internal color as the marbles swarmed through his life. It was glorious, and he was awake.

Each morning, the old man awoke and found a marble shining dimly on the floor near his bed. He kept his growing collection in the side pocket of his sports bag.

Sometimes, he took out the cookie tin and held Anouk's three, feeble marbles in his shaking hand. Only three stories of a life. *No wonder she inhabited the afternoon.*

On one of those afternoons, while the wind committed to the fall and the old man leaned out of room 23 window photographing the passersby, his shutters clicked across the salt-and-pepper head and slightly crooked nose of a slim woman encased in a blue wool turtleneck sweater, catching her in a leisurely, pensive stroll. Unaware that she had been photographed, the woman continued walking slowly for two blocks, watching the city blow past her in the smog and late leaves. Not far from the old man's hostel but out of range of his camera or his old eyes, the woman saw a marble in the gutter and, on impulse, she bent and picked it up. It was gritty and, to her surprise, warm to the touch.

> My name is Anouk, and when I was sixteen, I had what I believed to be a physical experience of the divine incarnated in my body ...

Startled, the woman opened her fist and allowed the marble to fall. She resolutely resumed her walk, ignoring the curious eyes of a small, fat woman dressed in pink seated in a nearby bus shelter, and within another two blocks had convinced herself that nothing untoward had occurred. The marble rolled into a drain, where it lay softly reflecting the daylight in a shallow pool, bemusing a family of rats.

CHAPTER 14

In Sydney, junk mail gathered and bunched in the old man's mailbox—discounts on pizzas, video rentals, Thai takeout, and offers to value his property. The local butchers had produced a new magnetized calendar, despite the fact that the New Year was still a few months away, and decorated it with a picture of an outback Australian landscape. They were pleased to offer it to the old man *free*, they boasted. Into this colorful array of literature, the postman occasionally stuffed a letter from the old man's telephone network, reminding him that his line rental of $28.89 and one call of $0.24, plus tax, were overdue. It rained, and the mail poking out from the tiny mailbox slot pulped. Into this, the postman pushed another bill, this time from the electrical company. The junk mail began to bulge out the other side of the mailbox, spilling onto the cement. At 4:00 PM on a rainy Thursday, the postman pressed into the already damp stack a blue envelope marked "Airmail." There was no room, and the letter remained half in and half out of the box, the black ink of the address, "Mr. G. L. Solomon," slowly blurring in the downpour.

Nobody came to collect the old man's mail, and nobody read the one real letter, which slowly crumpled and smudged and ran with the rest of the paper in the tiny box, rotting, over time, into a mess of color.

CHAPTER 15

At noon on a Thursday, the Pink Tracksuit and the old man engaged in a complicated kind of waltz, spinning each other around the giant ball that was Manhattan, heads resolutely pointed in opposite directions, but each oh so conscious of the other, their fat and ancient toes surprisingly nimble. Neither seemed to tire, though the dance had carried on for more than a week.

The old man rested by his window, camera in hand. *Click.* The crown of a tall, slender redhead was frozen. *Click.* The bright swirls of a crocheted Rasta hat, framed by dusty stumps of dreadlocks. Among the crowd, a fat, black woman in a pink tracksuit ambled in the old man's direction. At times, she glanced up at the window, smiling. *Click. Click.* Pause. *Click.* The old man photographed one after the next of the crowd surging under his room. Just ahead now, having passed by only moments ago and once again avoiding capture by camera, a pink, velour-clad bottom wobbled away.

The old man kept finding marbles in the street, especially around Midtown. True, he had trained his old eyes to see them; they were fine-tuned to respond to the quick flash of glass in the sunlight despite the transformation the marbles gradually underwent, dulled by months of dirt and smog and grease. Some were just plain marbles, lost debris of a child's forgotten game, but most belonged to Anouk. She was alive and inhabiting the entire lower half of the city.

At 3:00 PM on a Friday, the old man found two marbles in the long grass on the verge of the park at Union Square, right next to the farmers' market, and he made the mistake of picking them both up at once. They burned in his palm and both began at the same time.

> My name is Anouk, and I ignored my wealthy and much-beloved auntie when she became sick …

> My name is Anouk, and when I was three, I had a near-death moment, a drowning that …

> —not speaking to her for five years before she died so that nobody would think I was angling for a place in her will …

> —even all these decades on, I can remember as a covetable peacefulness, swallowing water and slowly floating down—

—when she died, I was overcome with remorse and knew, inside, that I had killed my love for her, not out of nobility, but pure laziness, a despicable pretence at superiority.

—surrounded by the soft blue, and thinking, in my mind, what a clever child I was for not panicking.

The old man sat down heavily in the wet grass, nauseous, but he did not let go of either of the marbles. The stories carried on, and together, the mixed-up words merged into something almost fleshlike in its humanity.

From somewhere within the park, there was laughter, a hearty chuckling that swelled into guffaws and thigh slapping. Nobody seemed to notice or not notice the nondescript woman in the pink tracksuit clutching at her ample, quivering sides, and the old man had things to listen to closer to hand.

At 2:00 PM on a Saturday, the old man left the lobby of his hostel, waving cheerily to the staff on the front desk, all of whom grinned back. The hostel had a general rule that guests could not stay longer than a week. They extended the policy for the old man first out of sympathy, and now they overlooked it because they loved him too well to let him go. He had long since ceased paying for board, which was a blessing, since his minimal funds came only from the HSBC bank account he set up upon arriving in New York, into which good old Mario deposited his pension check every fortnight. Nobody, least of all the old man, thought to question Immigration.

The old man turned right when he got to West Broadway, not to follow any plan or aim for any destination, but simply because the thinning fall sun was stronger on the southwest side. Trundling just head of him, unnoticed, an overweight black woman in a pink tracksuit squinted in the glare. When the old man ran out of interesting things to look at on his walk, he took a left-hand turn and crossed through the honeycombing Tribeca back streets. An hour later, he wound all the way back to Washington Square Park. He gratefully eased his tired body onto a bench and lazily watched the squirrels gather the last of their winter supplies. Next to him on the bench, a short, chubby woman threw the squirrels peanuts from a paper bag.

"Hello," the old man offered her.

The woman grinned but said nothing.

The old man took a breath as if to speak, but he swallowed it instead. After a moment, he glanced down at the veined hands resting on his knees. He frowned, but it was impossible to tell whether he did so out of irritation or puzzlement. The woman left soon after and quickly disappeared into the afternoon crowd.

An hour later, in the dimly lit back room of a nondescript bar on Bleeker Street, Pink Tracksuit eased her ample behind onto an oversized cushion in a crowded room. She watched and listened while others cast marbles into the center of the floor, and unwitting storytellers exposed their internal organs.

The moon was high in the sky and visible from the back room window when at last the final story trailed off. "Well?" demanded someone from the other side of the room.

"Success!" The Pink Tracksuit smirked triumphantly. "He's got years in him, too, and who would have known it? Worth losing a bet for, that one. Somebody pour me a glass of wine!"

There was a general cheer around the room, and the atmosphere of teasing and conviviality visibly swelled. Someone uncorked a couple of more bottles of red, and people eagerly held glasses up from the cushions.

"How about you, Dan?" the Pink Tracksuit asked.

"Listen and learn," came the cheerful response. He cast a blue and green flamed marble into the center of the room, and a story began.

"I was eating croissants and jam in Phuket the hot morning after Christmas when the ocean swallowed my lover. Snatched him literally from our table and digested him for brunch …"

"Ooh!" The group in the room was palpably impressed. They fell silent and let the story tell out.

CHAPTER 16

The old man decorated room 23 with all the photographs he had taken from above. Slowly, they covered one full wall—and then another. Karl had long since moved on in his adventures, but the new roommates who came and went so quickly were always accommodating to the strange old man. They loved to look at the photographs and bring their friends inside to study first one person's head and then the next. Some of them, like Karl, would draw the old man into their worlds.

Gradually, the old man began to recognize some of the heads and trap their routines in his camera. Dog walkers, models, cleaners, waiters. They came and went under the old man's lens, and he captured them all. One of the most familiar heads was blond and full haired, belonging to a man. It passed by almost every day. And once, when the head looked across the street at exactly the moment the old man took the photograph, it revealed thick, wavy sideburns. The old man came to know the head's stride, a firmly upright lower back, but roundness to the shoulders, a stoop to the neck, and a slow, measured walk.

By carefully studying the ground inside the photograph, the old man could tell that the blond head belonged to somebody tall. He watched, through the lens, the blond head walk toward him—shutter click—and the head was past. Try as he might, the old man could not glimpse the face beyond the sideburns.

But when he processed and posted on the wall twelve photographs of the blond man's head, the old man put away his camera and crossed onto the north side of Houston, because he knew the blond man's name.

> A boy named Joseph buys my drinks at Café Dante. That's this place with a lot of rules. You know, things like "no dogs" and "no laptop computers" and "cash only," et cetera, et cetera. It's where Bob Dylan used to go to write poetry and music and be inspired, so I go there to soak him up. So does Joseph. He has bushy, strawberry-blond sideburns that almost grow into his mouth. Joseph is an intellectual with a capital *I*, and writes philosophical papers for his class at NYU that I don't understand. Sometimes, when I read them, I frown and look thoughtful and make "hmph" sounds or suddenly yell, "Yes!" and startle the people in the café so that he thinks that he and I are on the same page.

The old man sipped his Café Dante drip coffee and grimaced. "The coffee is terrible," he remembered she had warned. She was right. And here were no poets or musicians or artists or intellectuals. Here were just a bunch of tourists and a handful of pretentious New Yorkers with too much money and too little to do to be working on a Tuesday afternoon.

The old man looked up. A blond man sat down at the table in front of him and grimaced over his own cup of terrible coffee. His face was young but very unattractive. Enlarged pores lumped and reddened his face, mixing with acne scars to create a thick, oily covering for his skull and neatly blending with his rather bulbous nose. On the other hand, the bushy, luxurious, strawberry sideburns covered much of the bad skin, and Joseph's chapped lips were full and sensual.

Of course, the old man knew it was Joseph. Joseph handed the old man a marble. "I believe this belongs to you," he said. "But you didn't have to throw it so hard," and Joseph rubbed his head. The marble in the old man's hand was warm to touch.

> I began my life at seventy-three, a baby in an old man's body, and my birthing slap was a letter from a stranger ...

The old man slipped the marble back into his pocket.

Joseph said, "You are here to find R———."
The old man replied, "Her real name is Anouk."
Neither the old nor the young man noticed a short, black woman in a pink velour tracksuit slurping coffee with gusto at the table next to them.

CHAPTER 17

The old man and Joseph sipped their horrible coffee, heads pressed close, piecing together the story of the stranger.

Joseph told the old man about his visits to Anouk. How he had found her in her apartment after having been missing for almost a week, hungry and unwashed, writing letters on letters and filling the lines in between the words with more letters. How, several months before this, she had appeared in Joseph's life as a regular face at Dante, carrying her Australian accent defensively and keeping her history close to her chest.

"She consumes people," Joseph said. But he said it with admiration.

The old man told Joseph about the letters he started receiving many months ago from a stranger in New York. Letters that detailed her initial explorations of the city, dark hints at secrets, memories of an unnamed man, always attended by acid or tears. He told Joseph about the first time the stranger noticed the Pink Tracksuit, and how, after the Pink Tracksuit had become the central antagonist in each of the letters, the old man received an extraordinary epistle. "I am writing to you from the Other Side." He told Joseph about the stranger's marbles sent, he presumed, by the Pink Tracksuit herself.

And then he told how, now that he had stepped at last outside of his narrow, routine-ridden world, his own marbles began to conceive and multiply. "My stories keep me alive," he said.

"'My stories keep me alive,'" repeated Joseph, and he stared hard at the old man, his watery eyes now sharp and excited and his forgotten coffee cold. "'There is nothing in this physical world that has not first existed in the world of ideas,'" he quoted. "'We are shadow puppets reflecting a brighter reality.' That's Plato," he added. "What I mean is … what if her stories, those marbles you hold, are the ideas or memories that enable her existence?"

There were several moments of silence. Joseph's question hovered in the still, Dante air. The old man stirred sugar and cream into his second cup of intolerable coffee, watching his own thoughts thicken and turn caramel like the drink. "I have always known her real name," he said softly. His voice cracked like an old man's, and he and Joseph both understood.

"The secret link," Joseph leaned forward conspiratorially, and the old man brushed spittle from his cheeks. "Because you don't exist in her past. Without even knowing she was doing it, she created for herself the perfect escape. By reading her letters, you have kept her alive."

"She must have given up," the old man said.

"She hasn't given up. She's just confused."

"No, not Anouk," said the old man. "The Pink Tracksuit. Why else would she send me those three stories that drew me across the world and into this extraordinary adventure?"

Why else, indeed?

Unnoticed, the short woman at the table next to them got up and left the café, readjusting the drawstring of the pink tracksuit around her wide behind and chuckling softly as she walked away.

CHAPTER 18

The fat woman in the well-worn pink velour reclined on cushions still scattered across the wooden floorboards. These, in daylight, were a lot dustier and dirtier than they appeared at night. Nobody else had arrived, and a small bowl of marbles sat still and silent in a corner, not cast and not played. The woman closed her eyes and smiled softly. Though her body seemed relaxed, the woman's very fingertips tingled with adrenalin, anticipating G. L. Solomon's destiny. The Pink Tracksuit's smile widened, and she opened her eyes. So, the old man and the ugly boy were beginning to understand. What would they do next? She couldn't wait to hear their stories …

My Dear Anouk,
    My name is G—— S——, but you know me better as Mr. G. L. Solomon. You will notice from the stamp on this letter that it was posted on the island of Manhattan, where I now reside.

I wish to thank you for your letters. It may not have been your intent, but your uninvited stories from this side of the globe enabled me to see beyond my own green walls for the first time in a very long time. You assisted me to once again view the world as a place to inhabit, not just exist in. If I sound overly poetic, you must excuse an old man's fancies. I have recently experienced an awakening somewhat akin to a rebirthing experience, and I am left more than a little off-kilter from the process.

Now, I believe I can help you. But before I put to you my suggestions, I feel it may be beneficial to tell you a little more about myself. I know so much about you—and yet so little of what is ordinarily known of a friend—but you know nothing of me except my name.

Firstly, I am aware that you are considering the possibility of getting a cat. I do not recommend this course of action. Cats are selfish animals that live only for their own comfort and to create allergies in others. I do not believe that a lazy, domesticated creature will be able (or willing) provide you with the salvation you need.

On another matter, though, I must agree. The coffee is terrible. I am yet to find a New York barista who can make a decent espresso, although your friend Joseph assures me that he has found the very place and will take me there shortly. Yes, Joseph. You have a true friend there.

I am presently an old man, although I believe I am growing younger. I was born in 1935, and I am sure you are capable of making the necessary calculations.

By the time I was old enough to go to war, it was over, but I spent several decades preparing for the next one. Not as a soldier, but as an observer. I make an excellent, thorough, fastidious observer. As a young man, I gained an apprenticeship with a local newspaper and, in time, became a writer for the *Sydney Morning Herald* in the grand old days of true journalism, complete with caps and cigars and brash words and fast-talking girls. First, I observed society parties for my paper, and then sports results, and later politics. And I wrote about them all, although apparently not particularly well. My editors could not find anything approaching a Hemingway in me.

In 1964, I obtained a passport, ready to be sent on assignment wherever the action would take me, and I diligently renewed it every decade. Until this year, it remained clean of stamps.

I failed as a writer and a political observer, and after six months of only moderate effort, I failed as a husband. My half-year marriage was in 1963. It may surprise you to learn that my beautiful wife, Ingrid, was Italian. Her father, it seemed, stayed in Germany during the war and was deeply enamored with the country despite the dark times, so much so that he persuaded his country wife to bestow a northern name on their brown little girl. Ingrid came to Australia on a boat with her parents in 1961. They couldn't afford to fly. In March of 1964, Ingrid's parents sailed back to Italy, their dreams dissolved in our soulless city, and Ingrid left with them.

It was after my marriage failed that I obtained the passport, but, of course, I did not follow her. For her second journey, Ingrid packed the smart clothes she had carried with her three years earlier but left behind most of her Sydney wardrobe. She took all the various cooking utensils and accoutrements that had littered our small flat, and she took our small child, who was three months in her womb.

You will think this is a tragic story of a lost child and a lonely man looking for his roots, but it is rare that I think about either of them. To me, Ingrid was a beautiful dream that, when I had married her and she became real, transformed into a constant strain of cultural misunderstandings, linguistic minefields, and financial hardship. The laughter and passion and warmth that had once been ours became, after it was made permanent, smoke.

As for the child, to me, it was never born. Ingrid was ill not only in the mornings, but all day, and she was unhappy and withdrawn. I can recall wondering how she would last the long sea journey back to Rome when she was so constantly sick on land. The child, to my mind, was purely a virus that has now surely passed.

You are wondering why I tell you these things. It is merely for you to understand why, in time—a failure—I chose to live my life inside, although of course until now you did not know I did it.

As J. Alfred Prufrock once said via T. S. Eliot, "I have measured out my life with coffee spoons." I comprehend his meaning. I, too, once measured out my life in tea bags and timings …

Enough. Now to your problem. You will be pleased to know that I am the bearer of several of your stories. From them, I believe we can reconstruct your life. I believe I have also uncovered the mystery of the woman who has been haunting your afternoons. As much as you are a character in her story, so she—by placing herself there—is a character in yours. And this gives you a godlike power, if you will but take it—the storyteller's choice. Cleverly, you have given her the slip, and it is now time for you to write her out of your next chapter. She no longer holds you. The tables have turned, my dear. You have played this game remarkably well.

Please give my regards to Joseph during his next visit. I am sure he will be able to assist you in this endeavor, because he, more than most of us, understands the nature of existence and its opposition to what we perceive as reality. He will also bring you some more writing materials, as I hear you are running short.

I, in the meantime, will continue to observe.

Cordially yours,
G—— Solomon

THE NEWEST MARBLE

At last, Anouk's pen was shocked into silence.

The old man's letter was unexpected and extremely unwelcome. What was Mr. G. L. thinking, entering—she could say *invading*—her quiet, private existence? And what did he mean by imposing his personality and history on her, building flesh of his own in letters where the only flesh should be hers?

Anouk's hand blindly stroked a cat that had joined her in the eternal afternoon. The cat closed its eyes but did not purr. Outside, she could hear it well; the children were playing marbles again. Someone had just won a bounty, and the others were not happy.

She thought about the Pink Tracksuit. She could almost see the woman smirking secretly, as though nothing and no one could be more innocent or guiltier. When and why did the Pink Tracksuit allow the old man to find her? Or had she? And how had Joseph and G. L. come to meet?

From the window drifted chatter and the *click, click* of marbles rolling against each other. A new game had begun.

Timidly, from the right-hand corner of the window, Anouk watched the children play. They weren't scruffy or gray as you would imagine children on the Other Side to appear, and their voices didn't echo with a sing-song mystery. They were laughing and swearing and wore fashion brands on their shoes. Modern children taking an old-fashioned game and making it their own. A craze that comes and goes and comes again.

Elastics. Anouk had liked elastics. White, ribbed bands wrapped around the ankles of two girls while a third jumped left, right, over, under, across, criss-cross, on top, in gymnastic weightlessness. Singing, swinging girlhood chants ... I went to the market to buy a fan. *Clap-clap. Clap-clap.* And who should I see but the draper man. *Clap-clap. Clap-clap.* Stomp on the left. Lift. Stomp on the right. Leap, criss-cross. Puff.

Elastics had been her favorite.

Then came marbles. Marbles had been the boys' game, and Anouk, loving the glass beauty but unable to participate, had purchased her own bag of twenty from the local toy store for $2.40.

Was it then, seduced by their mystery, that she had started to tell her stories inside balls of glass? She didn't know. She only knew she had loved the dark moons, spiraling spiders, paint-splattered galaxies, and flame-filled jacks and had at some point written herself into their worlds, creating stories for their impossibilities while she rolled them in her little hands and fed her memories to their misty insides.

Her father gave her three chipped marbles—a tiny jack, a red spider, and a milky moon were all that survived of his own childhood collection.

Anouk had a flash of understanding. Somewhere, now, the Pink Tracksuit and her friends were playing cosmic marbles with human stories. The outcomes, the winners, the losers, the collections, were all determined by the flick of a wrist, the mood of a god, and the slope of an immortal pavement.

This was the meaning of life.

She was not on the Other Side. She was simply part of a collection lost from the hands of a not very skilled marble player. One with unfortunate taste in fashion. And in that moment, Anouk understood what Mr. G. L. Solomon suggested in his letter. To win back her stories, all she had to do was play.

The letter had arrived not in a simple airmail envelope like the ones Anouk had used to write to Mr. G. L., but in a padded kind of cardboard mailbag. Still thinking about the Pink Tracksuit, Anouk felt back inside the bubble wrap lining, and when she felt the dozen or so marbles taped to the bottom, some of them chipped and dirty, she was hardly surprised. She freed the marbles and held them in her hands. Rushing through her, she felt pieces of her history finding their places and lodging once again in her bones as they grew inside her flesh.

All of a sudden, she filled with energy and life and mischief.

Anouk ran to the window. She was two stories up from the children playing their game on the pavement immediately below her. She ran to the kitchen (she had a kitchen! How long had this been here?) and filled a plastic jug with water. She walked it back over to the window and heaved up the sash. Aimed, tilted. The bulk of the water cascaded over one boy's head, but droplets splashed and surprised several others. They leaped about in the icy street, yelling. Anouk ducked below the window, crouching against the wall and suppressing giggles while she hid.

Two minutes … five. The children's angry cries had softened, and everything outside was quiet. She was about to peek out of the window again when *whoosh*! Something spun past her face and burst onto the far wall near the door, sending the cat screeching into another room, claws flailing on the floorboards. It was a water balloon, blue and broken on the wall. Anouk laughed. Outside, the children cheered in triumph. *This would make a story*, she thought, and everything flushed.

Water balloons, marbles, cats, pink tracksuits, stalkers, storytellers, airmail to a past life, letters from a stranger, sideburns, spaghetti, poetry, bad coffee, the city, the traffic, the pavement, the chase, the fall, the spill, the loss. Children's stories and building blocks, journeys, a fetus or two, a tearing, a grand passion, a frozen lover, a femur, the word "yes."

Mr. G. L. Solomon, apparently an old man, playing marbles in New York City.

* * *

A new game had begun, so Anouk decided it was time to desert her death and get up. When she did, she saw balloon debris and a water stain on the parquetry near the door. And in the puddle, there was a small glass marble. She picked it up, and it felt warm. It, too, lodged its story inside her bones.

There was a knock at the door. It was Joseph's ugly face and luxurious sideburns.

"Hello, you."

"Hi, Joseph."

"It's you again. You're back."

"It's me. I'm back."

"How are you feeling this morning?"

"Better. Is it morning?"

"Don't you know?"

"It's been a long time."

"Since what?"

"Since it was morning."

"You look better."

"I feel better. I need a drink."

"At this time of morning?"

"Especially at this time of morning."

"Let's get out of here, then. This place stinks of cat piss."